D0396085

Appendix A

Writings by Dr. Keith Anderson

Allegory of the Web

After our last storm I looked out my living room window and watched a spider begin to repair her wind torn web. To me, it seemed an impossible task. All that remained of her old home were a few strands of silk stretched across the corner of the window pane. But, she began. With almost painful patience she slowly ran strands of silk not more than a quarter of an inch long. With such diligence and intensity she worked, unaware of people and things around her. One link at a time, she'd slip and fall, drop a little–saved only by a silver thread of silk (woven by herself)–and then climb back to the web to string another link.

Two hours I watched! And I got bored. Her efforts seemed so tedious. I wondered, did she ever think how redundant her task must be, storm after storm, link to link, only to see her net torn again by wind and rain? I think she would have had hours to contemplate the futility of her efforts—in good weather, hours of quiet solitude and aloneness, waiting for her web to work, the self-doubt, the feelings of discouragement, lost visions, and shattered hopes. And then the storm—to rip her web to shreds. I think she would find it hard to weave again. But no, this spider, the one outside my front room window, she, with grace and dignity (even as she hung suspended from her web), with nobility and courage of royal blood, set to her task again. I like to think she never said a word of complaint or ever asked for thanks or even understanding.

And for all her effort?

I checked her web today—another winter storm. Though it still resembled her latest work of art, it stretched, torn and tattered, somewhat humbled by forces greater than itself. But, nonetheless, intact. What was missing was the spider. I checked the crevice she usually hid in, to wait for some unsuspecting fly or moth, neither was she there. A tiny hint of sorrow suggested itself to me. I thought, old age, the storm? Maybe a frightened visitor killed her to protect himself from her vicious attack. I thought, with a flush of anger, what a waste! I turned to walk away and never give this spider another thought. As I turned, I noticed four cocoons packed neatly in the corner of the sill. I can imagine this spring, a thousand tiny spiders, rushing with excitement to build a web, just like mom's.

My Mother the Prostitute, My Father the Pimp: A Study in Reaganomics

I was raised by parents who went through the Great Depression. I've heard many stories about that time. My parents worked very hard. They were middle class Americans, with middle class values and a middle class income, paying middle class taxes. My father was very responsible; he fished salmon in Alaska and milled timber in Washington. He was so worried about paying his bills that he would pay his utilities in advance.

We heard about conservation before it was popular, not because of natural resources, but because it cost too much to waste the water and lights. Even in the '50s we didn't go on Sunday drives because gasoline was expensive.

My mother sent us to confirmation and Sunday school and taught us what was good and right. She encouraged us to go to scouts and to do well in school, then we could become successful. She worked in the fish cannery in the summer to supplement our middle class income, and so she could spend money on school clothes for her children. It was important that we were well dressed and clean, and never tardy or absent without a good reason.

My parents were both very responsible people. They tried to raise responsible children. They voted for Ronald Reagan.

I remember the first time I saw Ronald Reagan. It was on "Death Valley Days." I didn't like "Death Valley Days," but my parents thought we should learn what a great country we lived in and what a great history it has and what great people made it such a great country. I still don't like "Death Valley Days" (except, of course, for the mule teams on the advertisement).

My father almost retired this year from the plywood mill. He didn't make it though. The mill closed down. Something about interest rates and inflation and budget cuts. He was a little worried, but what Ronald Reagan said about all the jobs in the newspaper made him feel better. He got a newspaper and made a lot of phone calls and drove to a lot of places and asked if he could have a job. It cost him a lot of money to be told they didn't need him. My father was sixty-four years old.

Because my father believed Ronald Reagan, he didn't give up. He went to Seattle. He went to First Avenue. Because my father has worked hard all of his life he is still strong and still looks young. Because my father was a father, a lot of young girls who had to leave home because of budget cuts and inflation and high interest rates want to help him. He wants to help them, too. They work together in Seattle to make money.

My mother wants to help, too. She's 4'10" and weighs 150 pounds. She's fifty-seven years old and has had four children. It's a little bit harder for her to make money, but she tries real hard.

Because they work so hard to see that their children do what is good and right, they won't accept part of our unemployment check. They say we need it to raise our own families. I think they might be too proud.

We don't go visit them much anymore. My mother says there isn't room in their Seattle tenement apartment. I think it's because of the fleas and cockroaches. Even at Thanksgiving and Christmas we don't get together. My father says it's the busiest time of the year and both of them have to work late at night. They don't complain though. They trust Ronald Reagan because he knows what he's doing, so do all of the other government people. They're even thankful because he is spending so much money on defense, especially on holidays, because then they see more sailors from the pier and more soldiers from Fort Lewis.

Sometimes I think they might like to retire and stay in a warm middle class home and visit with their grandchildren like they dreamed of when I was born. But they don't complain. They know that Ronald Reagan is doing the right thing. After all, he told us all about America on "Death Valley Days."

Affluent Society

When a generation of people feel it is not their responsibility to educate its successor, then is the time to review our values. In our "affluent society," the voting age generation has decided that it cannot or will no longer support the education system. In light of these materialistic values, I can see no reason why the abortion laws of Washington cannot be repealed.

If "the people" feel human life is not worth molding, at any cost, then what is its worth in making—only the satisfaction of the designers? It is apparent that money and mundane desires weigh heavier on our scales than an educated youth. If we cannot afford to school our spouse, we cannot afford to feed them. Abortion should not only be legal, but it would be immoral to allow life to continue under these conditions.

If the human being is not worth our money to educate, and our "affluent society" cannot sponsor any new members, then destroy them before our greed prolongs their destruction.

Legalize abortion or reform our schools.

Appendix B

Fishing by Season

1997

F/V *Sunny C* – Captain Larry Deck – Salmon

1998

F/V *Ten* – Captain Barry Northcutt – Salmon

1999

F/V *Ten* – Captain Barry Northcutt – Salmon

2000

F/V *Alaska Ocean* – Captain Scott Symonds – Pollock

F/V *Ten* – Captain Barry Northcutt – Salmon

2001

F/V *Alaska Ocean* – Captain Scott Symonds – Pollock

F/V *Ten* – Captain Barry Northcutt – Salmon

2002

F/V *Alaska Ocean* – Captain Scott Symonds – Pollock

F/V *Break Point* – Captain Steve Jacobson – Salmon

2003

F/V *Alaska Ocean* – Captain Scott Symonds – Pollock

F/V *Susan B II* – Captain Nick Mavar, Jr. – Salmon

2004

F/V *Miss Colleen* – Captain Nick Mavar, Sr. – Salmon

2005

F/V *Blue Adriatic* – Captain Brian Mavar – Salmon

F/V *Nuka Island* – Captain Norm Lennon – Cod, herring

2006

F/V *Blue Adriatic* – Captain Brian Mavar – Salmon

F/V *Mark I* – Captain Dave Bethell – Crab

2007

F/V *Blue Adriatic* – Captain Brian Mavar – Salmon

F/V *Northwestern* – Captain Sig Hansen – Crab, salmon, cod

2008

F/V *Blue Adriatic* – Captain Brian Mavar – Salmon

F/V *Northwestern* – Captain Sig Hansen – Crab, salmon, cod

2009

F/V *Blue Adriatic* – Captain Brian Mavar – Salmon

F/V *Northwestern* – Captain Sig Hansen – Crab, salmon, cod

2010

F/V *K2* – Captain Brian Mavar – Salmon

F/V *Northwestern* – Captain Sig Hansen – Crab, salmon, cod

2011

F/V *K2* – Captain Brian Mavar – Salmon

F/V *Northwestern* – Captain Sig Hansen – Crab, salmon, cod

2012

F/V *Northwestern* – Captain Sig Hansen – Crab, salmon, cod

2013

F/V *Kiska Sea* – Captain Mike Wilson – Crab

F/V *Northwestern* – Captain Sig Hansen – Crab, salmon, cod

Acknowledgements

This book would not be possible without the help of my friends and family. Thank you to my wife, Jenna; my mom, Donna; my sisters, Megan, Johanna, Wendy, and Beth; my uncle, Chris Anderson; and my aunt, Cami Mavar, for believing in me and having faith that I could achieve great things. Your help collecting pictures and remembering my past has allowed me to write this book.

Thank you to my brother-in-law, Devon Léger, and wife, Dejah, for your guidance during the earliest stages of this project. Your selfless contribution of time and advice has been invaluable.

This book would not be complete without the pictures provided by Casey Rigney, Matt Bradley, Sig and Norman Hansen, Jessie Elenbaas, Scott Harder, Erik Hammerstrom, Eric Lange, Alec and

Brian Mavar, Dan Murdock, and Ben Staley. Your pictures helped bring my words to life and allowed me to tell my story much better than I ever could on my own.

Thank you to my teachers, Patsy, Andy, John, and William Crawford. You have each guided me through my professional career and your mentorship has meant so much to me.

Finally, this book and more importantly my new life, would not be possible without Scott Moyer, may he rest in peace.

Jake Anderson
Seattle, Washington

Photo Credits

Index

CPSIA information can be obtained at www.ICGtesting.com
Printed in the USA
LVOW10s2321220714

395594LV00011B/182/P